For

Samuel Cyrus David Ray
from
his Godparents. St. Timothy 1976

THE MILKY WAY

THE MILKY WAY

And Other Chinese Folk Tales

ADET LIN

Illustrated by Enrico Arno

Harcourt, Brace & World, Inc., New York

Acknowledgments

All these stories are from traditional Chinese folk-lore. The following are based on published versions in Chinese collections and have been retold: "The Mason's Marriage," "How the Miser Turned into a Monkey," "Winter Rose," "The Egg," "The Golden Calf," and "The Old Lady and the Monkeys" from *Min Chien Tung Hua*, Pei Hsin Book Co., Shanghai, 1932; "Through the Eyes" from *Min Chien Ku Shih*, Pei Hsin Book Co., 1933; "The Boy Who Played the Flute" from *Min Chien Tsü Shih*, Pei Hsin Book Co., 1933; and "Growing Wings" from *Erh Tung Shih Chieh* Magazine, Vol. 18, No. 3, 1926.

CONTENTS

THE MILKY WAY

here were once two egrets and a little tortoise who were very good friends. They lived by a lake and played together, sunning on the sand and swimming in the clear water. When the graceful white egrets flew in the sky, the little tortoise would look up and laugh merrily, though he could not fly himself. They were together all the time and led a happy life by the lake.

One year there was a great drought. From March to August not a drop of rain fell. The rivers dried up, the lake grew smaller and smaller until finally it was nothing but mud, and after several weeks under the hot sun even the mud became dry and cracked. All the people who lived by the lake gathered their bundles and left. The egrets and the tortoise sighed and worried, especially the tortoise.

One evening the two egrets flew very far away. When they came back, they told the tortoise, "Everybody is moving to Silver Lake. It is two hundred miles away. Even the moles are tunneling their way toward it. We must leave, too." All the animals and insects were fast disappearing from the marshes. The lake was becoming an impossible place to live in.

The tortoise shook his head in sadness. "How shall I ever move fast enough? And I am so thirsty already."

The egrets said, "If we don't move from here soon, we will surely all die of thirst and hunger."

The tortoise wept pitifully, and the egrets themselves could not hold back their tears. Another day passed, and the change of weather they had hoped for did not come. The sky was bright, and there was not a sign of rain.

When the hot sun came up in the morning, the sobs of the little tortoise were fearful to hear, and he said to the egrets, "We have been such good friends. Can you think of a way to take me along?"

The egrets put their heads together. After some time they said, "Brother Tortoise, we have a plan. We are not sure it will work . . . but—"

The eager tortoise could not wait for them to finish and asked, "What is it? What is it?"

"We will hold the ends of a stick in our beaks, and you can hang on to the middle. This way we can fly high and fast, carrying you between us. What do you think of that?"

The tortoise was so happy, he nearly jumped. "That's a fine idea. Let us start at once."

The egrets were happy too, but they gave him a serious warning: "You must be very careful not to open your mouth on the way."

"I will keep it shut, even if someone tries to pry it open with a knife," replied the tortoise.

The egrets and the tortoise searched long and hard to find enough food to fill their stomachs and a little water, and early the next morning they said good-by to their home. Each egret held an end of a stick in his beak, and the little tortoise gripped the middle with his jaws. Thus the team took off and flew high over forests, glittering snow-covered mountains, and temples with gleaming golden roofs. The little tortoise had never felt so wonderful or seen so much in all his life.

Down on earth the poor farmers were trying very hard to irrigate their land, turning the water wheels and carrying pails of water to the fields. The children of the farmers pointed to the sky and shouted, "Look, look! What a clever tortoise! He holds the stick in his jaws and lets the egrets carry him." The egrets flew on as if they had heard nothing, but the tortoise glowed with pride. Everyone was praising him.

More children pointed as the friends passed overhead, and the farmers themselves looked up and laughed. The children watching cattle on the hillside clapped and pointed. "How wonderful! How smart of the egrets! They carry the tortoise to the

sky. We would like to fly that way, too." The children jumped up and down, but the egrets paid no attenion and kept on flying. Only the little tortoise felt very hurt.

"Look at the sky! The clever egrets are transporting the tortoise in the sky!" the grownups and children said all along the way.

The little tortoise puffed and huffed. "Stupid people!" he thought to himself. "Saying it's the egrets that are clever. It was really *I*, the tortoise, who thought up the plan. I am the smart one. I must let them know." Then with all his might he began to shout down at the people, "Hey! . . ."

Of course, as soon as he opened his mouth, he fell like a spindle through the sky and hit a rock.

"Oh, what a foolish tortoise," the people said. "Poor, stupid tortoise." And the egrets were very sorry, too.

nce upon a time there was a mason who went to work in a rich man's house to repair the roof. When he was working, perched up high, he caught sight of the rich man's daughter. She was very beautiful, and the mason decided he wanted to marry her. When he finished his work and went home that night, he told his mother of his wish. His mother said, "You must be crazy. You are only a mason. Do you think a rich man will let his daughter marry someone like you?"

But the mason could not forget the image of the rich man's daughter and kept thinking about her, whether he was working or eating, until his mother could not stand him any longer. So one day she called the matchmaker to see if she could arrange this match. The matchmaker was a goodhearted and ample-looking woman, and when she had heard the story, she went reluctantly to the house of the rich man.

"Are you willing to let the mason marry your daughter?" she asked the rich man.

The rich man sat in his chair, patted his stomach, and replied, "Certainly I am willing, if he will bring me four treasures."

"What are these four treasures?" the matchmaker asked.

The rich man laughed and said, "A strand of red hair three yards long, a one-footed golden cock, a three-legged frog, and a pearl-that-glows-in-the-night. If he brings me all these things, I will give him the hand of my daughter in marriage." The rich man had a good laugh. Who could ever find such things?

When the matchmaker told the mason and his mother the conditions for the betrothal, the young man decided he must travel to the Sacred Temple in the west to ask help from Buddha, for where would he get these four unusual things? His grandmother had told him before she died to go there and pray to Buddha if ever he should be in need.

So, early the next morning, the mason bade farewell to his mother and set out on his journey. He walked all day, and toward evening, at sunset, he stopped at a house by the road to ask for lodging. There were only an old lady and her daughter living in this house. They asked him in and inquired, "Where are you going?"

"I am going west to seek instructions from the Buddha at the Sacred Temple."

"Will you carry a message for me too?" the old

woman asked. "Please ask why is it that my daughter cannot utter a single word," for her daughter was dumb and could only shake her head or
nod when spoken to.

"All right, I will ask Buddha for you," the mason
said, and the next morning he bade them farewell
and continued on his journey. He walked through
many fields and traveled many miles.

That evening the mason stopped at the house of
a wealthy lord. After giving him a nice meal, his
host asked, "Where are you going?"

"I am going west to ask help from Buddha."

"Will you take a message for me, my friend?
Light an incense stick and ask why there is not
a grain of rice left in my granary, though I filled
it full last fall."

The mason said that he would gladly carry his
message and ask Buddha for him. He stayed over-
night and the next day traveled on, across fields
and hills.

Toward evening on the third day he stopped at a
farmer's house. The farmer took him in and also
asked where he was going. The mason gave the
same reply.

"Ask something for me too, since you are going
to the Sacred Temple," said the farmer. "Why is
it that all the water I put into the cistern at night
always disappears by morning? I cannot understand it."

"Farmer, I will ask that for you," the young man replied. He already had two messages to carry besides his own, from the old lady and the wealthy lord. He left the farmer's house after the night and proceeded on his way. It was high noon when he came upon a broad river, and there was no boat in sight to carry him across. As he was standing there, wondering what to do, a large snake raised its head from the waters.

"Snake, snake," the mason called. "Can you take me across?"

"Yes, I can," the snake answered. "But where are you going?"

"I am going west to seek instructions from the Buddha."

"Will you ask a question for me too? Why is it that I have been in this river five hundred years, and have behaved properly, but have not yet become a spirit?"

"I will inquire about it for you," the mason replied. "Please take me across."

The snake took him across the wide, ripply river on his back. Bidding good-by, the mason went on his way, across uninhabited land and through silent forests. That night, under the Big Dipper that glittered in the sky, he saw before him a magnificent temple with slanting roofs and many statues. This was the temple his grandmother had told him about. He went in, and kneeling before the statue

of Buddha, he confessed his wish and also presented
the four messages. Being very tired, he lay down
and fell asleep at the foot of the statue.

In his sleep, he had a dream, and in it Buddha
came to him and spoke thus.

"Young friend, the old woman's daughter cannot
speak because there is a red strand in her hair. Pull
it out, and she will talk. A single-footed golden
cock sits beneath the granary of the rich man. Take
away that cock, and the granary will not be emptied
of itself. The water in the cistern in the farmer's
field disappears because there is a three-legged
frog hiding underneath that drinks from it. Chase
the frog away, and the water in the cistern will remain. The snake in the river has been well behaved
indeed. The reason he has not become a spirit is
that on his head is a heavy pearl-that-glows-in-the-
night. Pluck this out, and he will fly away and become a spirit."

When the mason woke up in the morning and
recalled the dream, he knelt and thanked Buddha
again and again and started on his way home.

At the river's edge, the big snake was waiting on
the bank for him.

"Good day, what news have you brought me?"

"Buddha said there is a pearl on your head. Pluck
it out and you will become a spirit."

The snake carried the mason across the river

and then asked him to pluck the glowing pearl from his head. At once the snake flew to the sky.

Carrying the pearl, the mason went on until he came to the farmer's house in the evening. The farmer welcomed him, gave him food and tea, and asked, "What of my message?"

"Buddha said there is a three-legged frog underneath the cistern. Chase him away and the cistern will remain full." When the farmer and the mason went to the field and heaved up the stone over the cistern, they discovered a three-legged frog, true to Buddha's words. The mason asked his host if he could take this frog along, and the farmer was glad to get rid of it.

The next night the mason lodged at the wealthy lord's house. The lord said to him, "Surely, traveler, you have forgotten my message."

"No, I did not forget. Buddha said that beneath the granary hides a golden cock. Take away the cock and the grains in storage will not be touched."

The wealthy lord was very grateful, and under the flooring of the granary he found, indeed, a one-footed golden cock. When the mason asked to have it, the lord was happy to give the golden cock to him as a present, since it would save his grains.

Carrying his three treasures in a bag—the pearl-that-glows-in-the-dark, the three-legged frog, and the one-footed golden cock—the mason finally came to the old woman's house the next evening.

The old woman greeted him at the door and said, "Hello, so you have come back. Did you have a good trip? Have you any messages for me from Buddha?"

The mason replied, "Let me rest, and I will tell you. Buddha said there is a strand of red hair in your daughter's hair. Pull it out and your daughter will speak."

The old woman really found the red hair, three yards long, in the head of her daughter, and she pulled it out. They were very happy that evening, as the daughter was at last able to speak. When the mason asked for the strand of red hair, they were only too glad to give it to him.

With the four unusual treasures, the young mason arrived home very happy.

"Did you get all four things?" his mother asked him.

"Yes, all four." He brought them out to show to his mother, and told her the story of how he got them and about the people he had met on the way.

Then the mason took the four gifts to the rich man. Never thinking that the mason would find these strange things, the rich man now could not go back on his word, so he gave the young man the hand of his daughter in marriage and his blessing as well.

And that was how the mason married the rich man's beautiful daughter.

nce there was a simple cowherd who lived in a hut near a village in the province of Kiang-su. He planted and tilled the soil for the farmers, and when he was through with the day's work, he would take his water buffalo to graze in the pastures and on the hillside. So the people in the village came to call him only by the name of the Cowherd.

One summer day the weather was so warm that there was a heavy mist in the fields. No one could see clearly ten feet beyond, and it was so hot that all work stopped. As usual, the Cowherd took his water buffalo to the pasture, and he himself sat on a high spot on the ground, taking it easy, while the gray old buffalo grazed. The afternoon was quiet and the trees seemed asleep, when, quite suddenly, the water buffalo called to him, "Master, Master! At the end of the pasture there are seven fairy princesses bathing—near the bend of the river. If you will go there and snatch one set of clothes, you will have a fairy princess for your wife."

When the Cowherd heard this, he sneaked quietly to a cluster of trees by the river, and indeed there were seven fairy princesses with long hair bathing in the water. They were the loveliest girls he had ever seen. They laughed and chatted, unaware that someone was watching them. There, on the riverbank, were seven sets of clothes. Oh, what magnificent robes they were, with pearls and embroidery! One was pink, one light purple, one a golden yellow—all the clearest and brightest colors. They shimmered as if they were woven of dew-covered cobwebs.

The Cowherd went over and took up the set of clothes nearest him and hid again behind the trees. When the seven fairy princesses finished their bathing, they dressed, and—one after another—flew up on a cloud to the blue sky from which they came. They lived in a crystal palace high above, which was hidden from view.

But the youngest of the fairy princesses was left with no clothes to wear, and without her magic garment she could not fly up to the sky and return home with her sisters. She was lost and did not know what to do. When she saw the Cowherd, she tried to hide herself and at the same time begged him for her clothes, for she saw that he had stolen them, since he had a small bundle under his arm.

"My name is the Spinning Maid," she said to him, "and I am one of the seven heavenly sisters. The weather was so warm, we came down to bathe in the river and did not think anyone would see us."

Indeed, it was such a quiet and secluded spot shaded by willows, not even children or farm animals strayed there.

"Please give me back my robe so I can go home," she pleaded.

"I will get you something to wear," the Cowherd replied. And he ran back to the thatched hut where he lived. There he buried the magic robe of the fairy princess, got a blue cloth jacket and trousers, and hurried back to the riverbank.

There was nothing the Spinning Maid could do but put on the cotton jacket and trousers he brought her, and since she had no place to go and could not go home, the Cowherd took her home to his thatched hut, and the Spinning Maid became his wife. Since the Cowherd was a nice boy, she was quite happy and content.

As the days went by, she cooked and washed and kept house for him, and since she was very good at spinning, she also spun wool and cotton. Her husband tilled the fields and looked after the water buffalo and was very happy. And thus they lived peacefully for many months. Only every once in a while the Spinning Maid would ask where her robe was, but the Cowherd would never tell her.

One day the Cowherd found his old water buffalo lying on the ground, panting, and he went over and touched his back and patted him. The old buffalo looked up with sad eyes and said, "My time has come, Master. I am grateful to you for taking such good care of me all these years and never mistreating me. When I am dead, Master, you must pull off my skin and make a sack from the hide. Then fill it with yellow sand and tie it with a string. If you are ever in trouble, carry this sack over your back. It will help you." Not very long after, the old water buffalo drew his last breath. The Cowherd was sad to lose his old friend but did as he was bidden, taking the buffalo hide, making a sack of it, and filling it with sand. Then he buried his old friend properly.

A year passed, and the Spinning Maid led a contented life. She drew water from the well and scrubbed clothes, and she loved the Cowherd dearly, but every now and then she missed her sisters and asked the Cowherd where he had hidden her robe. Pretending that he had not heard her, the Cowherd always talked of something else.

Thus three years went by. The Cowherd and the Spinning Maid had a boy and a girl, and both were nice-looking children. The Cowherd was very happy.

One day the Spinning Maid said to her husband again, "Tell me where my robe is, the one I came down to earth in. You must tell me. I just want to see it."

The Cowherd thought to himself that surely by now the robe, which he had buried beneath a stone slab in damp ground, would be rotted, and since they had two children whom the Spinning Maid loved dearly, he was doubly safe. So he told her where he had hidden it.

When the Spinning Maid heard this, she flew to the spot. She dug only a few spadefuls, and there lay the robe, not stained or ruined, but shining with a wondrous light. She put it on, and as soon as she tied the jeweled girdle, she started to fly upward toward the sky. Looking down, she waved sadly to her husband and their two children. She was, after all, a fairy princess who must return home.

The Cowherd wept, and the little boy and girl cried too and called for their mother. How could they go after her? Then the Cowherd remembered the buffalo sack, which the old buffalo had told him to use in case of need, so he got the sack, slung it across his shoulder, and—carrying a child in each arm—found himself rising above the ground too.

Traveling through air, he pursued the Spinning Maid. And thus the Cowherd and his two children traveled for a day and a night.

When finally he caught sight of the Spinning Maid, she was already across the Great Milky Way, which divided the sky like a river of a million stars. The Milky Way was too broad to cross, and besides, the buffalo bag, which was not well stitched together, now gave out and all the yellow sand trickled down. The Cowherd had to remain on this side of the great river.

When the Spinning Maid returned to the Crystal Palace, she was welcomed joyously by her sisters, and once more she resumed the life of a fairy princess. Yet she thought of her family too, and she often brought her spinning wheel to the edge of the Milky Way so that the Cowherd and her children could see her working.

And the Cowherd? There were tilling and planting for him to do in the sky, and he took care of their children. He did not want to go back to the earth again.

One day an angel, who looked after human affairs as well as the lives of the fairy gods and princesses, was passing by and took pity on the separated family. He went to the Chamber of Sacred Books and pored over the Book of Destiny. He read there that the life of the Cowherd and the Spinning

Maid together was not yet over, so he devised a
way that they would be reunited once a year, on the
seventh day of the seventh moon.

On that night the Spinning Maid could cross the
Milky Way on her golden hairpin, which would
be transformed into a bridge, and the family would
be together for that one evening.

And that is why often on the seventh of July, if
you recollect, it rains in the early evening and then
the whole sky turns radiant and clear, for on this
night the Cowherd and the Spinning Maid meet
again. They cannot help weeping over the year's
separation, but then they spend the happiest night
of the whole year together.

And on all the other evenings, if you look up at
the sky on a clear night, you can see a bright star
twinkling on one side of the Milky Way, and on the
other side another bright star with two little stars
beside it. These are the Spinning Maid working at
her spinning wheel and the Cowherd minding
their two little children.

hina is a very large country, in which there are many cities. In one of these, Hangchow, there lived a long time ago a well-to-do couple. They had a brick house. Now Hangchow was a very beautiful city with its West Lake, and all kinds of people lived there. It was full of poets, beggars, and rascals, families large and small, singers, seamstresses, and merchants.

Though this couple were well to do, they were stingy and mean. They never gave money to the poor, they never invited anybody in for a visit, and they never helped anyone in trouble. Even on holidays their front door would remain solemnly shut, while there might be green willow branches on the neighbors' doors for the Dragon Boat's Festival, or cut-out red-paper decorations for the New Year, and firecrackers popping everywhere in the city. But all was quiet at their home. They never spared a "hello" or a friendly word for their neighbors, whom they considered unworthy of such courtesy.

As they did not have any children of their own, they bought a slave girl when she was twelve to do all the housework. She toiled from dawn till late at night, cooking the meals, scrubbing and washing, and doing everything for their comfort. Things had to be done just right, too. The slave girl worked all day, and at night, utterly exhausted, she would climb into her cot in the little broken-down bamboo shed behind the house. Of course she was never allowed to go out.

Naturally, this couple did not own a dog or cat, as it would be a great waste to feed an animal. But in one respect they were not stingy at all—with words. Whenever a beggar came to their house, he would get nothing but a long string of scolding words, such as "You ragged rascal! Why don't you go off and die somewhere? Go beg for a coffin and bury yourself. You eyesore, filthy flea bag! Are you blind, coming here to beg?" and so on, and so on. (Indeed he was a fool to go *there* to beg.) Thus they would shriek awful names at the beggar and finally chase him away with a stick.

The slave girl's name was Mai-erh, which means "Plum" in Chinese. If she did not clean the dishes well, or if she left a corner of the floor unswept, or disobeyed their slightest wish, or was slow in bringing them tea, they would call her "Sour Plum,

Bitter Plum," and other unpleasant names. Of course, if she ever broke a dish or spilled some soup or cooking oil, surely a waste, her ears would be boxed or she would be beaten. Mai-erh used to thank heaven that she was strong and sturdy and could work and work and not get sick. Since all that anyone ever heard from this house were angry noises, the neighbors called the couple The Horrible Misers.

Mai-erh did her chores day after day, obeying all the orders given to her from dawn to dusk, without a minute's rest. Her hands were red and coarse. She wore old castoff clothes, which her mistress gave her, and she had only a broken comb. One day she sighed and said, "Oh, why have I been put in this house? Is it not enough that I work? Must I be scolded all the time? When will I ever be through with these days of hardship? Oh, pity me!"

She was kneeling before the earthen stove, feeding dry rice stalks into the fire, as it was the habit in Hangchow to use for kindling these stalks from which rice had been thrashed. There were usually some grains still stuck to the stalks, which Mai-erh would pick off and save. She had about a thousand of these rice grains, which she kept in some paper in her shed. She did not know why she kept them, but they were the only possession she had.

One of the fairy gods who lived on the mountaintop and who could travel fast as lightning from place to place, heard Mai-erh talking to herself. He watched over the people of Hangchow and already knew about the ill temper of this miserly couple, so he decided that he would go down and test the intentions of this household. Disguised as a dirty, crippled beggar, he hobbled to the house holding a stick and a begging bowl. He wailed in a thin hoarse voice, asking for food.

"Old generous Master! Old charitable Mistress! Have mercy! I have not eaten in three days. Give me food! Have mercy!" He called and banged loudly on the wooden door. It so happened that just then both the miser and his wife were out, and only the slave girl was home, sweeping the floor.

"Oh, have mercy! Save a life! I am starving to death!" The beggar wailed on so pathetically that Mai-erh went to the door and opened it, and was surprised to see what bad shape he was in. But she was too frightened to give him anything from the house, even leftovers, as the miser's wife checked and counted all the jars and pots and bowls each morning and night. But the beggar looked so wasted that Mai-erh was moved and fetched the rice grains that she had saved. She poured them into the bowl that the beggar held and said, "Go now quickly and cook these for yourself. Go before my master and mistress come back, or I will be in trouble." As she prepared to shut the door, the beggar held onto her sleeve and said, "Wait!" And he dug into his rags and brought out a clean snow-white cloth and gave it to her. "Charitable maiden, thank you for your kindness. Use this cloth to wash your face each morning, but take care and don't let anyone else use it!"

Mai-erh was greatly surprised—first, to see such a clean facecloth in the possession of a dirty beggar, and second, to receive it as a gift. She took it and was about to shut the door when, just then, the horrible miser and his wife came into view at the head of the street.

They caught sight of Mai-erh standing at the door talking to the beggar. As they approached, they had already begun to rebuke her: "So, you lazy worm! Once our backs are turned, you take the time of the day to chat with the devil. Get yourself in! Have you swept the floor? Do you have lunch all ready?" and so on. Mai-erh lowered her head and went inside. By the time the horrible miser had fetched a stick to chase the beggar away, the fairy beggar had already disappeared.

Of course, the miser's wife checked everything in the house at once but found nothing missing. Still, she gave Mai-erh a good beating with a bamboo stick and forbade her to answer any more knocks on the door in the future.

Mai-erh cried herself to sleep that night, but thereafter, every morning, she used the cloth that the beggar had given her to wash her face. Her

puffy, sullen, and plain face became whiter and prettier, and even her masters could not help noticing it. They were actually amazed at the sight of her and could not understand what was happening. Neither face powder nor soap was missing, and when they called her "Sour Plum," the name did not seem to fit any more. Strange to behold, after a few weeks Mai-erh had grown really pretty. Her masters sat up in their chairs, dumbfounded.

Mai-erh's clothes were still dirty, her old shoes were still caked with mud, her hands were still red and puffy, her hair was covered with soot, but her face had become pink and pretty.

The mistress came right out and asked her one day, "What have you done to your complexion, you thief?"

"Nothing," Mai-erh replied.

But the mistress could not let it go at that and asked her a hundred questions, to all of which Mai-erh either shook her head or replied in the negative.

However, under constant questioning, Mai-erh finally confessed that the crippled beggar had given her a facecloth when she gave him the rice grains from the fuel stalks.

"So!" Her mistress jumped on her. "So, you gave rice to the beggar. You should have given it to us, and you have been hiding things. Give us that facecloth at once!" The miser's wife pinched the slave girl's ear and would not let go. The poor girl then recalled with alarm that she alone was supposed to use the facecloth and nobody else. But it was too late now—she had to give it to her mistress. The miser's wife snatched it up and went away.

The miser's wife was secretly thrilled to have this magic cloth, and so was her husband. And they did not bother with Mai-erh the rest of the day or evening either.

The next morning both the husband and wife were very eager to use this facecloth to wash their faces, thinking that they too would become good-looking. But what do you think happened? As soon as they washed their faces with this cloth, short brown hair started to grow all over their faces and over their bodies too, and they turned into two monkeys. So they who had been so haughty became ashamed, and all they could do was run away to the mountains, and they never came back.

ne warm spring day everything was sprouting. The mustard greens were in bloom with their tiny yellow flowers. The birds were chirping, the farmers were busy planting rice, and the butterflies were already flitting about. It was also the time of year when one thought of such unusual things to do!

By the duck pond a farm laborer's daughter, a little girl about seven, was tending geese and crying. The geese were honking, but she would pay no attention and kept on rubbing her eyes. Along came the landowner's daughter, who liked to take a walk to see what was going on. "Hey, what is the matter with you?" she asked. "Why are you crying?"

The goose girl sniveled. "I am crying because—I'm sad I don't have wings. I would like to have wings."

"Stupid, of course you don't have wings. What do you want wings for?" asked the landowner's daughter, who thought herself very smart and who was really very curious.

The farm laborer's daughter, with her head lowered and still rubbing her eyes, whimpered. "I want to have two wings so that I can fly to the sky and sing, so that I can look at the moon up close and see all the hills and forests . . . so I can fly around in the air."

The landowner's daughter angrily told her, "What a foolish notion! Stupid, how can you hope to have wings? Besides, your father is only a day laborer. If anyone were chosen to have wings, I would be the one."

After her little speech the landowner's daughter walked off and marched over to the well. The idea of being able to fly appealed to her also. From the pail of water standing by the well she sprinkled some water on her shoulders, because water generally helps things to grow. Then she went and stood in the fields in the sun, waiting for wings to sprout.

Along the road came a merchant's daughter, all dressed up and with rouge on her face too. When she saw the landowner's daughter standing there with her face turned up, she asked, "What are you standing there for, little girl, you red-face?"

"I have decided to grow wings. I am going to fly."

The merchant's daughter almost doubled up with laughter. "Ha-ha-ha! You dumb country girl! You are daydreaming. If you grow wings, you will only add weight, but you won't be able to fly!" And she went on her way, snickering at the country girl.

But when she got back home to the city, she thought about it again and considered herself fit to grow wings. So she went and bought a bottle of olive oil and sprinkled some on her shoulders. Then this little girl also went and stood outside in the yard.

As she stood there, looking very silly, the daughter of a magistrate came by and saw her. "Little girl, why are you standing there?"

"Why, I am waiting to grow wings, of course."

The official's daughter, in a haughty voice, said, "Hunh, growing wings is not fit for such as you. It's for the aristocrats."

She lifted her head high and went home, and once she was in her father's sumptuous house, she got a pail of milk and had a milk bath. Then she went and stood outside in the sun, waiting for wings to sprout. Her parents looked at her strangely, but she remained fixed to the ground and didn't move.

It wasn't very long before the Princess of the Kingdom came by, followed by her retinue, and when she saw the magistrate's daughter standing there with her face turned up to the sun, she sent an attendant over to inquire what the strange girl was doing. The attendant ran back to report that the girl had taken a milk bath and was waiting in the sun for wings to sprout.

The Princess laughed shrilly and exclaimed, "What a stupid girl! She is wasting her time. Doesn't she know wings are only for a princess?" She pictured a pair of snow-white wings. So, of course, when the Princess returned to the palace, she sprinkled herself with the very best of perfume, went outdoors, and stood among the peonies in the Royal Garden of the King with her eyes closed. She was confident that wings would grow, since she was the Princess.

Well, in practically no time at all, all the young girls in China were standing outside in the sun with their faces turned up. They were getting sunburned, and nothing else was happening; yet they refused to budge or to do a stitch of work.

It was a ridiculous situation, and neither their fathers nor mothers could do anything about it.

The Spirit in charge of Wings who lived high above Mount Tai soon heard about this and flew down immediately to see what was going on. When he saw all these Chinese girls standing there waiting for wings to grow, he shook his head and spoke to them sternly, thus:

"Young ladies, if I give you all wings, and you all fly to the sky, who will stay home, obey their parents, and look after the younger brothers and sisters?

"I can give only one of you a pair of wings, and that will be the first girl who asked for them."

So he touched the farm laborer's daughter, who tended geese, lightly on the shoulders, and soon

after she sprouted wings and could fly to the sky at will. She liked to sing little ditties, and up and down the valley people heard her singing. Unfortunately, she did not sing very well.

And the Spirit in charge of Wings, when he saw that all the other Chinese girls had returned to what they were doing before, went back to his home on top of Mount Tai and resumed his duties of looking after eagles, hawks, sparrows, and the various other feathered creatures.

And, to be sure, the parents in China were very much relieved.

THE LAZIEST MAN IN THE WORLD

ow, I must tell you about the laziest man in the world, the like of which has never been heard!

He was a baby, a boy, and then a man. It was quite natural that he should be fed, clothed, and taken care of by his mother and father when he was a baby. But when he grew up, his parents certainly had a strange way of taking care of him— by letting him be lazy. To be truthful, however, there was very little they could do about it, or he could do for himself, for he was the laziest person in the whole world.

When they stood him up, he would lean against the nearest thing, be it a chair, a table, or a wall. When they brought him out to sit underneath a tree, he just sat there, come rain or shine, and he did not even care if a dog or a cat crawled over him and started to lick him or chew his shoes.

And, of course, to begin with each day, someone had to dress him and put his shoes on.

It was needless to ask, when he lay down in bed, would he ever get up if someone did not come along and start the whole business for him. He rapidly became known as the laziest person within fifty and a hundred miles of where he lived.

In this way he grew up; he got bigger and lazier each year until he was about twenty years of age. His parents even found him a wife from a distant and remote village. And she soon took over part of the job of feeding and caring for our hero. In the summer, when hot weather came, she had to wipe perspiration off his face and chase the flies away. And in the winter, when it got very cold, his nose would freeze if a window happened to blow open and someone did not come along to close it. So you see, his wife had much to do.

In a few years, when his parents died of old age and fatigue, his wife was the only one left to feed and clothe him. She washed, cleaned, cooked, and locked the doors at night against thieves, and opened the windows in the morning for the sunshine to come in. . . . She had a busy time.

One day the wife received news from home that her mother was very ill. Her mother lived in a village across the mountains that would take three days' journey to reach. The wife *had* to go home to see her mother; yet the trip would take a week even if she stayed only a day or two with her mother, and meanwhile her husband would starve to death! So she searched her mind and thought of a way. She got busy and baked about twenty biscuits, with a hole in the center. She strung them on a string like a necklace and put them around her husband's neck.

Then she propped the fellow up in a chair in the sitting room facing the front door, thinking if he were to stay in one position, it would be better that he just sat instead of lying down. At least strangers would see, if they tried to break in, that there was someone in the house.

Having placed her husband thus in a chair, with a string of biscuits around his neck, she then gave him instructions that he should eat one or two biscuits each day when he was hungry and said that she would be back as soon as she could. Her husband merely blinked his eyes once. So she left.

The wife went on her journey and visited her mother, and whether her mother got well or not is not important to us. The point is that when she came back in six days, she found that her husband had died of starvation, for he was indeed the laziest person in the whole world! He had eaten all the biscuits in front of him, yet the biscuits on his back were still untouched. He had been too lazy to pull the string around!

ould you like a silly story? Here is one.

There was once a wizened old man who lived with his wife on three acres of land. Usually what they planted on these three acres provided them with food and enough produce to exchange for the other necessities of life, such as clothing, kitchenware, material to patch their house, and farming tools.

Unfortunately, one year an oak tree started to grow on their land, and it grew bigger and bigger each day, until within one month its spreading branches and sheltering leaves covered the entire piece of land. The wheat, barley, and vegetables the old man had planted could not get any sunlight, and they all withered and died!

The old man decided he must cut down this tree, but it had already grown so big around that it was as thick as fifty or sixty trees! He went back and forth with his saw all morning and could not even scratch the bark, and already his forehead was covered with perspiration and his arms were sore! Yet if he did not get rid of this tree, nothing else would have a chance to grow, and soon he and his wife would starve to death. With this thought, the old man sat down sadly in the shade of the giant tree and started to cry.

From down the country road a young man who was walking along came up to the old man and asked, "Old fellow, why are you grieving?"

The old man shook his head and said sadly, "This strange tree has covered my entire three acres. Nothing else has a chance at the sunlight."

The young man flexed his muscles and made an offer. "I will pull up your tree for you, old fellow. But I am hungry, and you must feed me first."

"That is fair enough," the old man said. "Let me go home and have my wife cook you something to eat. How much can you eat?" he asked the young man.

"Oh, I don't eat too much," the young man replied. "Just make some porridge with—eh—a hundred-pound sack of rice, and make me a bun with —eh—two—hundred pounds of flour."

"What a big appetite!" the old man exclaimed to himself. "However," he thought, "since I am asking him to do something, I have to feed him properly." So he went on home, borrowed one hundred pounds of rice from his neighbor to the east, and two hundred pounds of flour from his neighbor to the west, and had his wife make a huge cauldron of porridge and bake an enormous bun. After his wife had prepared all this food, very wearily the old man brought out his oxcart to lug it to the young man. But on the way to the fields a very small woman, dressed in jacket and trousers, approached him and, looking upon the cartload of food, said, "Old fellow, I am thirsty. Permit me to drink some porridge."

The old man replied, "All right. You may drink a little." But what a surprise when the small woman drank up the whole cauldron of porridge, snatched the huge bun, and started to run away! The old farmer's jaw dropped open in shock, his eyes popped, and his two legs trembled and shook. When he brought the empty cart to the young man, the fellow naturally asked, "Where is my porridge? Where is my bun?"

But the old man was so dumbfounded he could not speak a word, and pointed a trembling finger at the fleeing figure of the little woman.

"Hrrumph!" The young man snorted angrily, brushed the crumbs (which were still considerable in size!) into his hands, and threw them into his mouth. They went right down his throat, and he said to himself, "At least a little bit to stave off hunger." Then with his left arm—*squeek-crash*—he pulled out the big tree, and with the tree, root and all, he started to chase after the little woman.

The fleeing woman, turning back, saw that she was being chased and sought somewhere to hide. But where could she hide? She looked all around her. In the open field there was only a farmer bending down, weeding with a scythe. So the little woman went up to him and pleaded hurriedly, "Farmer, farmer, help me! There's someone after me!"

The farmer stood up from his cutting and said, "How can I help you?"

The little woman replied, "Just open your eyes wide, and I will jump in."

The farmer made his eyes very wide and very big, and the little woman with one hop jumped into his right eye. But by then, the young man with the tree had already caught up with her, and he also leaped into the farmer's right eye.

The little woman ran from the right eye to the left eye, and the young man immediately followed her across the bridge of the farmer's nose. As a matter of fact, in the corner of the farmer's eye there was a square table where four little men were playing cards, with four little men watching, and all eight men stared at this strange commotion. However, by then both the little woman and the young man had leaped out of the farmer's eye, and she was already running down the road toward a mountain on the horizon.

The muscular young man was very angry, and

he stopped and picked up some pebbles and threw them mightily at the little woman.

But, alas, his aim was poor, and the pebbles did not hit her at all. Instead, they fell into a bowl of rice that an old woodcutter was eating outside his hut. He took a mouthful of pebbles and broke his front tooth! Angrily, the woodcutter called to his wife inside the hut, "Old woman, old woman, how careless you are! I told you to wash the rice carefully, and look! It's full of gritty sand." Amazed, his wife had no answer.

This is where this silly story ends, but nevertheless, as far as we know, the young man is still chasing after the little woman who ate up all his porridge and his bun. We don't know whether he ever caught her!

One winter it was exceptionally cold, and there had been heavy snow several times. At the foot of a mountain in a hut, a mother lay sick in bed, her face pale and worn, and her two daughters of eight and ten stood by her side. She was very weak, and when the doctor came to call, he said, "She must have soup made with fresh rose petals, and only then will she get well."

The two daughters loved their mother dearly and wanted to do everything to make her well, but they looked at each other. The wind was blowing loud and strong outside; where would they find fresh roses at this time of the year? They bundled themselves up and went out.

If the doctor had said pine cones, they could have picked them from the ground even in the snow. If he had said quince flowers, there were the chilly yellow quince flowers that bloomed in the cold.

The entire mountainside was covered with snow,

and all the weeds were frozen. The two sisters looked around and did not know which way to turn for blooming roses at this time of the year.

Then the elder sister remembered, and she said to her sister, "Do you remember last summer, one day, we went and saw some rosebushes in front of a cave? Maybe we can go there. That is our best chance." The younger sister agreed, and they climbed up the mountain, past the bamboo stiff with ice, and the tall pine trees, still green but aloof and shuddering in the cold. Up the steep path they went, struggling against the wind, and trudged on into a world of white. When they came near the cave that they had seen in the summer, the north wind seemed to subside, and the blizzard stopped. It was like a summer day, and a lovely fragrance greeted them. By the mouth of the cave there were bushes and bushes of red roses, and even a few bees buzzed about.

"Oh!" the two sisters exclaimed with joy, and they bent down and picked right and left. They picked and picked until they each had a big bunch of roses. How lucky they were, they said to themselves.

As they were turning to leave, something strong suddenly grabbed hold of each girl, and when they looked down, they saw they were each held by a hairy hand! It was a large, frightening hand that was attached to nothing, but it was very powerful.

The two hands were pulling the sisters into the cave.

They struggled to get away but could not get free. "Help, help!" they called, but no one could hear them, and they were dragged inside the cave.

They found themselves in a great stone hall. When they looked up in the dimness, there stood a black-faced hairy wizard as tall as the ceiling of the cave. Two huge green, luminous eyes stared down at them, and this frightening creature called, "Little devils! Now you can chop off their legs, and we'll see if they dare come again and pick my roses." Two little green-faced dwarfs leaped out from a dark corner of the cave, each swinging a big shiny sword, and within a fraction of a second they started for the two sisters.

The children cried, "No, no! We must tell you why we came! Our mother is sick, and she must have rose-petal soup to get well. That is why we came."

"Ha! What is that to me? How dare you tamper with my roses?" The wizard raised his very long arm and was about to ask the dwarfs again to chop the children down.

But both sisters pleaded, "No, no, you mustn't kill us! Our mother's sick and we have to take care of her."

"What is that to me?" boomed the wizard once more. The little dwarfs were ready with their shining swords.

"Stop!" the children called. "We must ask you

something first—then if you must, you can chop us down."

"What is it you want to know, you little fools?"

"We want to know who brought us in."

The large green eyes shone down from the height of the hall. "I did!" The huge, hairy wizard blinked, and he slapped his knee with satisfaction. He looked like a giant spider.

"We don't believe you, we don't believe you," the captives said.

"How dare you not believe me?" the wizard boomed.

"We don't believe you. You are fooling us because we are children."

The wizard grinned, showing all of his twelve protruding teeth. "Of course I brought you in!"

"But we couldn't see you at all," the sisters said.

The wizard demanded impatiently, "Is this all you want to know before you die?"

"Yes, yes," they replied.

"I'll show you," the wizard said proudly. "I have a long gown—it is an 'invisible' gown. When I wear it, you can't see me! It is a true treasure!" He laughed, and his laughter rumbled through the whole cave.

"There is no such thing. You are fooling us!" the children insisted.

The wizard let out his woody laugh. "I'll wear it to show you, you little fools." He turned around

and took from a peg on the wall a black gown.
He started to put it on to show off, but at the same
moment the two girls jumped and snatched the
gown, and in a minute the gown and the sisters
had disappeared!

The wizard roared as if someone had lit a fire
under him. He cursed and he stamped his feet. Not
being able to see the two girls, he bellowed
at his little devils, "Find them, find them, and I'll
kill them! The little thieves!" So the two dwarfs
swung their swords *whack, whack, clash* in the air,
but of course they could not see the little girls
either. The wizard roared some more until the
whole cave seemed to shake.

Hidden under the invisible gown, the sisters very
cautiously edged their way out of the cave. As
soon as they were outside, they picked more roses
hurriedly. In all the fright they had dropped the
bouquets they had gathered before.

Then one sister turned to the other and said,
"We'd better leave the invisible gown here. It
would never do if he traced it to our house."

"That would be terrible," agreed the other. "Let's
leave it here." So they dropped the strange black
gown at the mouth of the cave and, snatching
their bunches of red roses, ran downhill for their
very lives.

The wind started to howl again, and the snow
flurries came thick and fast. They wrapped their

scarves around the fresh flowers so they would not freeze. At last they reached home, puffing and out of breath, their feet and hands numb with cold.

In the house they boiled water, made soup with fresh rose petals, and served it in a bowl to their sick mother. After she drank the soup, she began to feel better, and when, the next day, they told her about their adventure with the strange creature in the cave, she hugged her two brave little girls gratefully.

The rose-petal soup was brewed every day, and the mother drank it every day. When all the rose petals were finished, the mother was well enough to get up and walk about, and the two daughters were happy indeed.

bout a hundred years ago, there lived a man and his wife who were neither very well to do nor very poor. As they were nearly forty and did not have any children, they were worried that they would not have an offspring. They decided to go and pray before a local earth-god that was supposed to be very helpful in granting wishes.

The couple went to the temple, and with great sincerity knelt before the statue of the earth-god and prayed thus: "Oh, Earth-god, we have been hoping for a son, day and night, and so far have not been granted this wish. You are a kind earth-god. Please help us. Please give us an heir."

Then they went home. Several months went by, and the wife became pregnant, but when the nine months were up, she did not give birth to a child at all, but to an egg, like a chicken egg! The weather was very cold, and the egg begged his mother to take him up and warm him, so she held him in her hands.

The husband and wife did not know what to make of it. They were torn between astonishment and disappointment. But at least, they consoled themselves, it was better than not having anyone at all. They took care of the egg as best they could, being careful not to drop him. In a way it was very simple. He did not create much trouble, and he liked to talk a lot, so he was good company for the couple. He was very affectionate, and sometimes he and his father carried on a conversation for hours.

One day the daughter of a wealthy family, who was an elegant beauty, strolled down the street in front of their house. At this time it happened that the father of the egg, with the egg in his pocket, was standing at the door looking out at all the hubbub going on in the street.

When the beauty strolled by, the egg called from the pocket, "Father! Father!"

"What is it?" his father asked. "What is it you want?"

The egg shouted, "I want that beautiful girl for my wife."

The father was taken aback and said, "Egg, have you gone crazy? What are you thinking? Do you want to lose your life? Stop shouting."

The egg, after being scolded by his father, started to sob and cry in the pocket. When the lovely lady in her flowing robe and high headdress had gone out of sight and the father had entered the house, the egg cried and cried without control.

He cried in the day and he cried at night. His parents were annoyed; yet they did not know what to do. Sighing heavily, they told him, "Egg, egg, you won't stop crying; yet it is completely useless. Have you forgotten what you are? How can you expect a beauty from such a family to be willing to be your wife?"

The egg replied quickly, "Father, Father. Please send a matchmaker and try. I am sure her family will say yes."

The parents were pestered without end by their unusual offspring and finally gave in. They sent two professional matchmakers to the rich man's house, and very boldly and matter-of-factly the matchmakers suggested a marriage between the rich man's daughter and the egg.

When the rich man heard this, he roared with laughter and answered jestingly, "Of course, of course, I will let my daughter marry such a one, provided he builds her a house with golden pillars and a jade roof and sends a sedan chair strung with sea pearls and gold beads to fetch her. Of course," he roared, "I will give my consent then."

The two matchmakers went back and dutifully

reported these terms to the egg's father. The egg was in his father's pocket, listening, and when he heard this, he felt very confident and answered the matchmakers directly. "Fine, we will accept these terms. But will I then truly have the consent of the father for the wedding?"

The egg's father was in complete despair and said, "How will we get the money to buy these things? You accept these terms—yet what am I supposed to do?"

The egg replied, "Don't worry, Father. I know how, I know how."

So the two matchmakers reported back that the egg's family had accepted these terms, and would the rich man therefore truly consent to the marriage? The rich man was surprised that what had started as a joke was accepted in earnest. He thought for a while, and gave his consent, and waited for a sedan chair strung with sea pearls and gold beads to come for his daughter.

Soon after, the egg's father said to his son, "So they have promised and consented, but how are you going to find these treasures?" He knitted his brows and pondered the question.

"Come with me, Father," the egg said, "and bring a hoe to our back garden."

The father did as his unusual son bade him, a hoe in one hand and the egg in the other, and they went to the back garden, which was full of fruit trees, bushes, and grass.

"Father, Father," the egg called. "Please dig into that weedy old grave in the eastern corner of the garden."

His father replied, "I can't, I can't! That is a grave over a hundred years old. How many ghosts must live there I do not know. We must not disturb them. You know, every spring and autumn we burn paper money for them."

The egg answered, "Father, you were misled by hearsay. That is not a burial ground at all, but a hiding place for old treasures. When there was a war, a wealthy man hid all his money and treasures there and made it look like a grave so nobody would disturb it and so he would remember the spot. But that wealthy man was killed and never came back to claim his possessions. The hoard of treasures is still there today."

When the father heard this, he dug open the old "grave" and found treasure of every kind.

With this they were able to build a house with golden pillars and a jade roof and to have a sedan chair made, strung with gold beads and sea pearls. Now they only waited for a propitious day to fetch and welcome the bride.

When the rich man heard that the egg was really going to marry his daughter, he was so frightened that he shook in the chair he sat in, and when his daughter heard that she was soon to become the wife of an egg, she cried as if she would draw her last breath.

And one day the sedan chair, carried by four strong men, arrived at the rich man's house, and the beautiful daughter was borne away.

In the new home of the egg, lanterns and colored silk streamers were hung over the mahogany and marble furniture in preparation for the bride. And before long the bride herself arrived, dressed in red, her head covered with an elaborate red kerchief.

The best man held the egg, who was now silent, in his hand. The bridesmaid took hold of the arm of the bride. They bowed to Heaven and Earth, they bowed to the father and mother of the house, and so the wedding ceremony was performed. At the wedding feast no one ate, so sorry they were for the bride.

Then in the bridal chamber, bright with candles and lovely with flowers, sat the bride, and on the bed was the egg. All the wedding guests felt great pity for her and wept silent tears of sympathy. One by one, the guests left, and the father and mother also retired to their own room, and there in the chamber remained the bride facing the egg. Neither spoke, and for a long time there was great quiet in the room. Suddenly a circle of red light appeared around the egg, the egg started to roll, the shell broke open, and out came a handsome young man. The bride was very happy.

But in the morning he went back into the egg again. And when the egg's mother asked the new bride, "Dear girl, how did you pass the night?" the bride hesitated at first and then told the truth. The mother said, "Why don't you crush the shell, if by chance you have the opportunity, so that the magic youth will remain always with us?"

The bride agreed and said, "Yes, my mother-in-law, tonight I will find an excuse and crush the shell."

Night fell, and the handsome young man came out again. The bride leaned on the egg shell and crushed it.

The young man, on hearing it crack, cried, "Alas, our marriage is over," and so saying, he vanished.

And thereafter the bride cried and cried, though she lived always in the house made of gold and jade and was well loved by the parents of her lost husband.

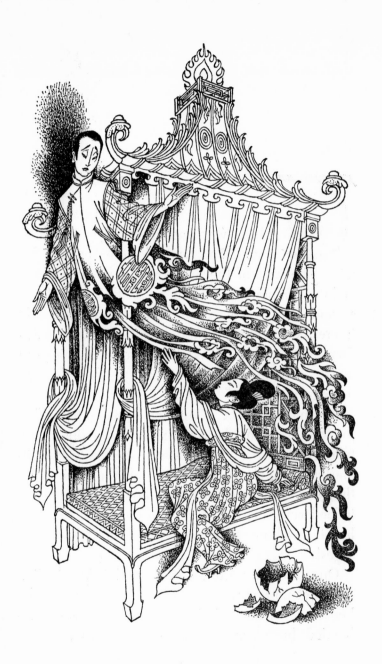

here was once a family with three sons. The two older ones each had a wife. The wife of the first son was not very good at housekeeping, and neither was the wife of the second son, who was somewhat sloppy and only interested in eating. So the parents talked between themselves and said, "We must have our third son marry a capable young woman so that she can manage the house."

In time they got a very good daughter-in-law for the third son. She could manage the house and take good care of the parents. She knew how to market, how to be frugal, and all the many little things necessary to running a household. She was indeed very smart. Everyone in the house followed her instructions as if they were words from the sages!

One day she posted a sign on the door, which said that no one was to enter the courtyard of the house empty-handed. People could leave empty-handed, but no one was to come in without something. If they had nothing to bring in, at least they could bring a handful of dirt.

It was a strange rule, yet the old and the young —man, woman, and child—all obeyed it. Whenever they had nothing to bring in, they brought a handful of dirt, until in a year or two there was a small mountain of it by the wall in the courtyard.

One day a wise man walked by the house and through the open gate saw the pile of dirt in the yard.

He said to the third daughter-in-law, who was standing by, "I presume you are not selling that pile of dirt. But if you were, how many ounces of silver would you ask for it?"

The smart daughter-in-law thought to herself, "How can this pile of dirt be worth anything? There must be a reason. I shall ask for one hundred ounces of silver," and that was the price she named.

The wise man said, "All right, let it be sold for one hundred ounces of silver. I will buy it."

When the young woman heard that this stranger was willing to pay one hundred ounces of silver, she was so surprised she couldn't believe her own ears, and she asked, "Why is it that you would pay one hundred ounces of silver for this heap of earth?"

The wise man replied, "There is a golden calf with a golden bell tied on a golden rope in the dirt pile. If you bring red beans and call *Mah-a-a!*

Mah-a-a! he will come out, and when he eats the beans, he will lay pieces of gold."

So saying, he reached in his pocket for money to pay her, but found none. "Ah, I will come back in three days with the money to claim the dirt," he said.

"Fine, fine," the third daughter-in-law replied. "I shall wait for you in three days."

After this strange man had left, the young woman took some beans in her hands, went before the dirt pile, and called, *"Mah-a-a, Mah-a-a!"* When she had called three times, the head of a golden calf emerged, and she kept on calling *"Mah-a-a, Mah-a-a,"* until the whole calf came out with a golden bell jingling on his neck. And when the calf ate the red beans, very soon afterward he laid pieces of gold.

Three days later the wise man came back, and the third daughter-in-law said to him, "Sir, you can give me a hundred ounces of silver now and move the dirt pile away."

But the wise man, who could tell many things we ordinary people do not know, said, "Alas, you have called out the golden calf. What use have I now of the dirt?"

They both laughed. The wise man did not buy the pile of dirt, and the golden calf remained with the family, which was overjoyed to have such a smart daughter-in-law.

THE BOY WHO
PLAYED THE FLUTE

Many years ago, in a tiny village by the sea, there were two brothers. When their parents died, the elder brother and his wife took charge of the younger brother, A-Ping. Since their circumstances were difficult and the wife had a mean and cruel nature, she did not treat A-Ping well at all.

One day she decided to get rid of him altogether and asked her husband to take him to a barren rocky island in the bay and leave him. There was supposed to be a fierce snake that ruled the waters there and ate people, and she wanted to leave the young boy to his own fate. Her stupid husband did not think for himself what was right and what was wrong and obediently took his little brother in a small boat to the strange barren island and left him there. Without giving A-Ping a backward glance, he rowed the boat back by himself.

A-Ping roamed the island. When he did not see his brother, he did not understand at first and was sure that the boat would come back for him. But he waited and he looked all day in vain.

The sky turned gray, the sea turned black, and he was all alone. He passed the cold night huddled in a crevice of a rock, and early the next morning he looked toward the ocean again for his brother, but there was no boat in sight. Sadly he sat down on a rock, and remembering how badly his sister-in-law had always treated him and the nasty way in which she spoke to him, he realized at last that they were leaving him on the island.

He dropped his head to his knees and sobbed, but being a brave boy, he soon stopped—and did not wish vainly any more.

He found that he was hungry, so he went about the craggy rocks looking for food. Fortunately he found some wild potatoes in the ground, and after washing them with ocean water, he ate them. When he was no longer hungry, he soon forgot the sorrow of his brother's abandoning him.

A-Ping had always loved to play the flute. Sometimes he played it all day without stopping, much to the annoyance of his sister-in-law. Now he took out his little bamboo flute, which he had brought with him, sat down on a rock by the water, and began to play little tunes.

The sun glistened on the ocean waves, and sea gulls flew hither and yon. The tunes he played were most touching. They sounded as brave as a hero telling of his battles, as sweet as a gentle maiden picking flowers, as full of joy as the small animals in the forest would be if all the tigers and foxes were gone. The flute told many, many stories.

Every night A-Ping curled up in a cave that protected him against the cold and mist. There were potatoes in the ground to sustain him, and soon he was making friends with crabs and crayfish that crawled up on the island. And he was content that he could play the flute all day.

One day, when he was playing the flute, an old man with a beard, dressed in a long robe and looking like a schoolteacher, appeared unexpectedly out of the waves. He called, "Good morning," and A-Ping, surprised, said in reply, "Good morning."

"Good friend," the old man said, "indeed you play a pretty flute. My young mistress has been listening to you every day. She says she has never heard such pretty music anywhere, and she has been anxious to come and meet you, but the old mistress that is her mother has forbidden her to come.

"Alas," the old man said with a sigh. "She grew unhappy and sick, and now she is lying in bed in a sick sleep. My master has dispatched me to invite you to play the flute for her, so that my young mistress may regain her health. He will thank you profoundly himself." After saying these words, the old man bowed.

It was a very unusual thing to have an old man appear out of the water, but when A-Ping heard his courteous speech and saw his gentle manner, he lost his fears and asked, "But who is your master?"

The old man beamed proudly and said, "Why, he is the most honorable Dragon King of the Ocean. Even on land you must have heard of him."

"Yes, I have," A-Ping said, nodding, and then he asked wonderingly, "Is it true about your young mistress falling ill? And in that wavy deep water, where do you live?"

"Why, in the Dragon King's Palace at the bottom of the ocean," the old man replied, pointing at the water on which he stood.

"It must be very deep down," A-Ping said. "I should be glad to go with you and play the flute. But though you may be able to dive and travel in water at will, how can I?"

"You can—the path is wide. You will see!"

"I shall surely drown," A-Ping said.

"No, be of good courage. Follow me, and you will be safe."

"Is it true?" the boy wondered again.

"Yes, yes! My master is very impatient, waiting for you. Bring along your flute!"

"All right then. Let us go . . ." Being of adventurous spirit, A-Ping jumped in after the old man and was soon beneath the water.

When A-Ping opened his eyes, he saw before him a wide avenue that was even and dry and paved with sand. At both sides of it there was blue-green water, with dancing seaweed and all kinds of fish swimming about. He and the old man could walk on the path easily, and they soon arrived at a magnificent building with turrets and ornaments made of shells. It was a palace fit for kings and queens. A-Ping was in great awe. At each side of the gate stood a sentry, formally dressed in armor and looking very serious, but the sentries' eyes protruded like a crab's.

They went in through the heavy gate, and the old man led A-Ping to a dark reception hall, politely excused himself, and went out. A-Ping looked about him. It was a large room. The walls were encrusted with pearls; the floor shone like gold. There were finely carved chairs with silk cushions, many tables with knobby silver feet, and on the tables stood various jewel boxes and vases. Indeed the whole place could not have been more tastefully or richly decorated. A-Ping was astonished.

With his bare feet and his cotton suit, A-Ping felt very awkward in the room, but he sat himself in one of the high straight chairs, and in a little while the old man brought in an elderly couple, who greeted him cordially. Both the man and the woman had white hair, and their faces were full of wrinkles; yet they had a most radiant expression, and their eyes shone with kindness and good spirit. Their manner was as spritely as if they were in their youth.

A-Ping stood up, for this was the Dragon King and his wife. They asked him to sit down again and in courteous words told him about their only daughter, who was now sick in bed. "Would you kindly help us save our daughter?"

"Yes, I shall be glad to play for her, if it will help her," A-Ping answered. They led him through a maze of corridors and halls until they came to the young lady's bedroom, which was beautiful, with silk curtains and furniture of coral. The bed was made of mother-of-pearl, and a heavily beaded curtain hung all around it.

A-Ping chose a stool and sat down. He began to play a song that he had never played before. The tune was melodious and soothing. As he played, the music floated through the beaded curtain to the Dragon King's daughter where she was lying in an unwaking sleep. But when she heard the lovely music, she suddenly sat up, opened her eyes, poked her head through the curtain, and said, "How well you play the flute! I am completely recovered. How can I thank you?"

Her parents were overjoyed at her recovery, and so was A-Ping that his playing had worked the magic. The Dragon King's daughter was very pretty, with shiny black hair and almond-shaped

82

eyes, and she was dressed in the prettiest dark green silk pajamas.

A-Ping got up, but the Dragon King, who was happy and grateful, insisted on his staying with them for a while and on showing him the whole palace.

The Dragon King took him first to his throne room, which was a magnificent hall with pillars of crystal and a gleaming throne made of abalone shells. On the floor was a rich rug of many colors. There were many rows of stools of all shapes about a foot high for all the Dragon King's courtiers and visitors.

The Dragon King then invited A-Ping to a banquet in the dining hall, where they were presently joined by the Queen and the daughter, who was now well. They sat down to a feast, which was served by a succession of fish standing on their tails, carrying in tray after tray of steaming food! A-Ping had never seen anything like it—or tasted such good food! After they finished the feast, they listened to an orchestra of twelve clams, of all sizes, that made the most foolish and the funniest noises! All A-Ping could do was listen politely.

The Dragon King then asked him about his life, and he told the King and his wife briefly how he came to be on the island. They listened with great sympathy and at the end invited him to stay with them. Their young daughter had fallen in love with A-Ping and wanted him to be her life companion. She was determined not to let him go.

A-Ping was very happy to have this invitation from the whole family, and after pretending some serious thought, he consented to stay in the palace for a while.

Every day he played the flute for the daughter.

And every day the Dragon King held court. There were all kinds of callers: lobsters, squids, whiskered catfish, and sea urchins, that came to the Dragon King with their disputes and asked him to settle them. Even the giant octopus came to the palace and behaved himself very well, withdrawing his tentacles and nodding at what the Dragon King had to say. He wished to move to a new home, but he was afraid of traveling. So the King assigned two lantern fish to guide him, on the promise that he would not eat them up or smoke them up with his black ink.

An oyster had a problem and came one day with knitted brows and a worried face. The Dragon King straightened it all out for him, and he floated away placidly without even saying "thank you." The Dragon King explained that oysters were sometimes like that, so concerned were they with themselves.

A-Ping learned how to swim in deep water, and he visited many silent and phosphorescent nooks and coral beds. But he was happiest in the palace, because the Dragon King and his wife were both very kind, and he also grew fonder and fonder of their pretty daughter. After a few weeks, to everybody's rejoicing, A-Ping and the Dragon King's daughter were married. You can imagine the guests that came to the wedding party!

Now that the Dragon King's daughter was married and her mother permitted it, A-Ping could take her out of the water to watch the sunset or walk along the pebble beach, and sometimes they hid behind a rock to watch the children shouting and playing.

One day A-Ping took her to visit the strange barren island, his old home. Before long, they saw a huge snake with something clutched in its jaw slithering across the water toward them. When A-Ping looked carefully, he recognized that it was his sister-in-law, with her hair hanging loose. In a faint, weak voice, she was gasping, "Brother, brother, help me." A-Ping wanted to help, but the huge snake had already slithered past him.

In a little while they saw A-Ping's brother rowing toward the island, calling, "Hello, hello! Have you seen my wife? Have you seen my wife?"

When he got near, he was startled to see his younger brother, whom he had thought long dead, looking healthy and happy. The two brothers embraced each other, and A-Ping had to tell him about seeing the snake go by with his sister-in-law in its

jaws. The brother wept. Then A-Ping told him all about himself and introduced the Dragon King's daughter. When his older brother heard this, he bowed his head, very much ashamed of himself. He began to sob again, feeling sorry for his lost wife and also for what he had done to A-Ping. A-Ping was also touched. After talking it over with the Dragon King's daughter, the couple invited the brother to return and live with them in the Dragon King's Palace now that he was all alone. The brother was grateful, but as he was frightened about diving, they each had to hold one of his hands, and then all three jumped in together.

So it came to pass that thereafter the brother too lived in the Dragon King's Palace and led a very lazy and contented life. Eventually he became treasurer to the King, just for something to do. But he never wished to leave the palace.

As for the young couple, they were exceedingly happy. They came up to the island often, and when A-Ping played the flute, the huge snake always stayed in the distance respectfully and listened to the music.

THE OLD LADY AND THE MONKEYS

There was once an old lady of about sixty, who lived all alone in a little hut. She planted carrots, and that was how she made her living. And she would sit all day long on a stool in front of her hut, wearing a hood to shield her head against the sun, watching, guarding her carrots.

One morning about twenty monkeys came down from the mountains and, with an awful racket, started to trample on the grass and to pull out all the carrots, except three little ones. There was nothing the old lady could do to stop them, although she got up and shooed them. They trampled everything, strewed bits all over, and, jumping up and down, threatened to come back for the remaining three carrots that night, just to pester the old woman. Giggling and hooting in turn, they went away gleefully.

After they left, the old lady surveyed the disorder, and then she sat down and cried.

"I'm ruined, I'm ruined! My carrot field is gone!" Being an old lady, she could not do much but weep and feel sorry for herself. She sobbed and sobbed, and whenever she looked at the ruined garden, she shook her head again and again.

Along the country road came a mat salesman on his way to the market. When he saw the old lady looking so sad, he asked, "Old lady, old lady, what is the matter? Have you lost your son? What is the matter? Did you have bad news?"

"No, no, but look!" She waved her hands. "I'm ruined! The monkeys came from the mountain and ruined my garden!" She pointed a trembling finger. "And they are threatening to come back tonight."

"Oh, what a pity," the mat salesman said with great sympathy. "Don't worry now, old lady. Here, take these three straw mats, and put them down tonight on your staircase."

"Now, why would I want to do that?" The old lady looked up, surprised.

"Do as I say," the mat salesman said, and gave her the mats. The old lady thanked him, and he went on his way.

After the salesman left, the old lady fell asleep with her hands in her lap. It was quiet in the countryside, with very little doing. Then, toward noon, a farmer came along carrying baskets of eggs on a pole on his way to the market. He put

the baskets down when he saw the old lady sitting
there with her head down, and called, "Ho, there!
Lao tai-tai [which means old lady]! What happened to your carrot field?"

"The monkeys came and tore it all up." She was
reminded of it again and started to moan. "And
they threatened to come back tonight."

"Don't worry, don't worry, old lady," the fellow
said. "Here, take this dozen eggs, and put them
on your stove tonight!"

"What would I want to do that for?" the old
lady asked.

"Do as I say," the farmer said, and he counted
a dozen eggs and put them by her side next to the
mats. The old lady nodded her thanks, and he went
away.

Still the old lady sat quietly, shaking her head
and saying, "I'm ruined, I'm ruined." And she did
not stir from where she sat.

In the afternoon the sewing-goods salesman came
along and inquired of her what was the matter. She
repeated the whole story, and this thread-and-
needle peddler patted her gently and said, "Cheer
up, old lady; take these pins and put them through
your mosquito net tonight."

"Why should I do that?" the old lady asked. "All
these foolish ideas!" she thought. However, she
accepted the pins, putting them with the other gifts,
and thanked the salesman, who went on his way.

The sun began to set in the west, and the old lady had to move indoors. She pulled the three remaining carrots and decided to take them with her. Tomorrow she would plant them right by her hut. She mumbled to herself, "How useless, how useless! My carrot field is ruined!" Then she picked up the gifts the three salesmen had left her and took them inside as well.

There was no moon that night, and after supper as she was about to retire, the old lady decided she might as well do as the three salesmen had told her, though it seemed utterly useless. She put the eggs the farmer had given her on top of the stove, the three straw mats on the staircase, and she put the pins through her mosquito net around her bed.

Along about midnight she heard a loud racket and a lot of animal chatter. The monkeys had come, a whole batch of them, to pester her and steal her last three carrots. They stumbled in the dark, not knowing which way to go, so they went to the kitchen to search for a light.

As they groped along, the eggs, which had been heating on top of the stove all this time, exploded and blinded six or seven of the monkeys. They let out a yell. The rest of the monkeys started to rush upstairs, but the mats were on the staircase, and they tripped on them, tumbling and somersaulting! There were only a few monkeys that managed somehow to get upstairs in the dark, and when they came to the old lady's bed and started to pull her mosquito net, their hands were pricked by the pins. They screamed and yelled, and ran and fell downstairs, and all took off to the hills.

So the old lady was unharmed, and the monkeys did not return to pester her again.